This book belongs to:

....

....

....

Stories

for

4

Year Olds

Written by Moira Butterfield,
Nick Ellsworth, Marcel Feigel, Kath Jewitt,
Jan and Tony Payne

Illustrated by Leighton Noyes
(Graham-Cameron Illustration)

Designed by Blue Sunflower Creative

This is a Parragon book
First published in 2005

Parragon
Queen Street House
4 Queen Street
BATH BA1 1HE, UK

ISBN 1-40544-720-6
Printed in England

Stories

for

4

Year Olds

p

Contents

One Balloon for Mickey

Mickey the bear woke up and rubbed his eyes. He knew that today was a very special day, but he just couldn't remember which special day it was.

"It's not Christmas," he thought, looking out of the window at the bright sunshine. "It's far too warm for that. And it's not Easter now. Easter was last week, and I got ten Easter eggs!"

He decided to wake his friend, Mops the mouse, who was still fast asleep and snoring loudly.

"Mops!" he shouted in his friend's ear. "Wake up! I want to ask you something."

Mops slowly opened his eyes and saw

Mickey's big face staring down at him.

"What do you want, Mickey?" asked Mops, who was still half asleep.

"I know that today is a very special day," said Mickey. "But I can't remember which special day it is."

"It's your birthday, silly!" said Mops, getting out of bed.

"My birthday! I'd completely forgotten," said Mickey.

"And all your friends are coming for your birthday tea," said Mops.

"Hooray!" cheered Mickey. "That means I'll get lots of presents."

"Of course you will," said Mops. "Now, I've bought all the food, but there's one thing missing."

"What's that?" asked Mickey.

"We haven't got any balloons," said Mops.

"But we can't have a birthday tea

without balloons," moaned Mickey.

"Then we'd better go down to the shop and buy some," said Mops.

Mops hopped onto Mickey's shoulder and they went down the road towards the shop.

"I hope it's open," said Mickey excitedly.

They turned the corner and saw the front door of the shop was open.

"Thank goodness!" sighed Mickey. "How many balloons shall we buy?"

"I think ten will be enough," said Mops.

The pair walked through the front door towards Mr Newton, the shopkeeper, who was standing behind the counter.

"Can I have ten of your biggest balloons please, Mr Newton?" asked Mickey politely.

"I'm very sorry," said Mr Newton. "I don't have any balloons left."

"But you must have," cried Mickey. "I need them for my birthday tea."

"I'm sorry, Mickey," said Mr Newton. "I sold them all earlier this morning."

"What are we going to do, Mops?" asked Mickey. He looked very unhappy as they walked out of the shop.

"I know," said Mops brightly. "There's a fair at the park. We'll be able to buy the balloons there!"

"Well done, Mops," said Mickey, and they started running down the road towards the fair.

"Hey, watch out!" yelled Mops, who nearly fell off Mickey's shoulder.

Mickey carried on running. As he got nearer to the park, he could hear the fairground music getting louder.

"Listen to that, Mops," said Mickey. "Isn't it exciting?"

"Remember," said Mops. "We're only here to buy balloons!"

Mickey wasn't listening. He was running as fast as he could through the park gates. Little Mops had to hang on even tighter.

The fairground had everything a bear would love. Fantastic rides, huge helter-skelters, all kinds of stalls and lots of places selling ice cream and candy floss.

"I think we should head straight for the balloon stall," said Mops.

But Mickey was walking towards a huge slide he had spotted.

"Oooh – look at that," he said. "It would be fun to slide down there."

"But we've got to buy the balloons," said Mops.

"Oh, please Mops," begged Mickey. "Please let me have just one go!"

"Well, all right then, since it's your birthday."

"Thanks, Mops," said Mickey happily. "You're my best friend ever."

After a long walk up many steps, Mickey and Mops reached the very top of the slide.

"Look how high we are, Mops. This is going to be the best slide ever."

Poor Mops had covered his eyes with his hands. It was far too high for him.

"Ready, Mops?" asked Mickey. "Here we go! Watch out everyone – here I come!" he yelled, jumping on.

"Wheeeeeee..."

he shouted on the way down.

"Wasn't that a great ride, Mops?" asked Mickey eagerly.

Mops didn't say anything. He was feeling a bit sick!

"Are you all right, Mops?" asked Mickey. "You look a bit ill to me. I think an ice cream will cheer you up."

He walked over to the ice cream stall.

"I'd like the biggest ice cream you've got, please," he asked the ice cream man. "What about you, Mops?"

"No thanks," said Mops in a little voice. "I'm feeling very sick."

"Are you sure?" asked Mickey. "They look really yummy."

Mops just shook his head.

"Oh, well," said Mickey, tucking in.

The moment Mickey had finished eating his ice cream, he spotted a merry-go-round. He ran over to it and jumped on a beautiful gold-and-white horse.

"But what about the balloons?" asked Mops anxiously.

"I promise we'll get them after this ride. Hang on! Here we go!" cried Mickey.

The merry-go-round started off slowly at first, then went round faster and faster.

"Whoaaa!" cried Mickey. "I feel like a cowboy. This is great fun!"

"I really enjoyed that," said Mickey, after the ride had finished. "How about you, Mops?"

But poor Mops was feeling sicker than ever, and didn't answer.

The two friends sat down on a bench, and after a while Mops felt a lot better. "I really think we should go and buy the balloons now," he said.

"I'd almost forgotten!" said Mickey. "Come on, let's go then."

When they arrived at the balloon stall, they found that the balloon man was packing up, ready to go home.

"Thank goodness we found you before you left," said Mickey breathlessly. "We'd like ten of your biggest balloons, please."

"I'm very sorry," said the balloon man, "but I'm afraid I've sold almost all my balloons. I've only got one left."

"Oh, no!" groaned Mickey unhappily. "But it's my birthday today and all my friends are coming to tea. It won't be the same with only one balloon."

"I told you we shouldn't have gone on those rides," said Mops.

"Oh dear," said Mickey sadly. "I suppose we'd better have that one, then."

Mickey gave the man some money, and the man handed him a large, bright-yellow balloon.

"It's lovely," said Mops. "What a shame we don't have any more!"

"It's all my fault," moaned Mickey. "We probably would have got a lot more if I hadn't gone on all those rides."

Mops felt sorry for Mickey. "Never mind," he said. "We'll play lots of games and have some delicious things to eat."

"I feel so upset, I'm going to have a candy floss to cheer myself up," said Mickey. He went over to the candy floss stall, and bought the biggest candy floss Mops had ever seen.

"You'll never eat all that. It's huge!" said Mops.

But five minutes later, Mickey had gobbled it all down. "Ah, that's better," he said, rubbing his tummy. "I feel a lot happier now."

"Good," said Mops. "Now, let's go home. We've got a lot of things to do before everyone comes for tea."

Mickey held on to the balloon very tightly as they walked back through the fair.

Suddenly, a gust of wind snatched the balloon from his hand.

"My balloon!" he yelled.

The balloon sailed high into the sky.

"What are we going to do?" cried Mickey.

"Quick, follow it!" shouted Mops.

"Hang on!" yelled Mickey.

He raced out of the fairground, with Mops holding on tightly to his shoulder.

The balloon was now just a tiny yellow dot in the sky.

"We'll never reach it," groaned Mickey.

"Of course we will. Just keep running," yelled Mops, bouncing up and down on

Mickey's shoulder.

They followed the balloon back up the lane and up the hill.

"I don't think I can run much more," Mickey puffed. "My little bear legs are getting very tired."

"We're nearly at the top," said Mops. "Don't give up!"

But when they reached the top of the

hill, the balloon was nowhere to be seen.

"Where's it gone?" asked Mickey.

"I don't know," replied Mops, puzzled. "It was there a minute ago."

While Mickey sat down to rest, Mops had a big think.

"I think I know where it might be," he said suddenly. "In the woods! Come on, Mickey. There's no time to rest."

Mickey got to his feet and, with Mops still sitting on his shoulder, ran down the hill and into the woods.

"It's a bit dark in here," said Mickey. "Let's go, Mops. I'm scared."

"Don't be so silly," said Mops. "There's nothing to be afraid of."

All of a sudden, Mickey spotted something horrible dangling from the branch of a nearby tree.

"Hey – what's that?" he said in a frightened voice.

"It's all right, Mickey," said Mops. "It's only a spider."

"Thank goodness for that!" said Mickey. "It looked like a really horrible monster."

They searched all over the wood, but they couldn't find the balloon anywhere.

"Now what are we going to do?" asked Mickey, slumping onto the ground.

"It must be somewhere," said Mops.

A gust of wind rattled the leaves up in a very tall tree. Mops looked up, and out of the corner of his eye saw something else.

"Mickey, look!" he cried, pointing excitedly. Stuck in one of the highest branches was the bright-yellow balloon.

"Hooray!" yelled Mickey. "You've found it!" He gave Mops a big bear hug.

"All we've got to do now is get it down," said Mops.

"I think I'd better fetch it," said Mickey.

"Be careful!" said Mops.

"Don't worry," said Mickey.

Mickey started to climb. Up and up he went until he was almost at the very top.

"Are you all right?" shouted Mops anxiously.

"I think so," said Mickey, standing on a branch. "I think if I really stretch, I can reach the balloon." He stretched out his arm and grasped the balloon by its string.

"I've got it!" he cried.

"Well done, Mickey. Be careful on the way down," yelled Mops.

But then, something terrible happened.

"Quick, jump!" Mops squeaked. "The branch is about to break."

Mickey grabbed the balloon's string, just as the branch broke. Hanging on to it tightly, he floated down to the ground.

"Thanks, Mops," said Mickey, hugging

him tightly.

The two friends made their way out of the woods, and were soon standing outside their house.

"I'm glad we found the balloon," said Mickey. "But it's still a shame we've only got one."

They walked up the path and opened the front door.

"HAPPY BIRTHDAY, MICKEY!" everyone shouted.

Mickey couldn't believe it. To his big surprise, his friends were already there, and they had filled his house with...balloons!

"So that's why there were no balloons at the shop or at the fair," said Mickey with a grin. "My friends had already gone and bought them all."

They played lots of party games and, when they were hungry, ate Mickey's birthday cake, which was made entirely out of...ICE CREAM.

Everyone played some more, until it was time to go home.

That night, a happy Mickey and Mops went upstairs to bed.

"That was the best birthday party EVER!" said Mops, closing his eyes.

"It certainly was!" replied Mickey, licking his lips.

The Hippso-Piti -Potimus

H olly liked to pretend. When it was warm and sunny she liked to pretend the paddling pool in the garden was the sea and the sandpit was the beach. When it was dull and rainy, she liked to play under the kitchen table.

When Holly was under the kitchen table she could pretend to be anywhere she wanted. She took her favourite things with her – her doll Rosemary and Corkscrew the clown, and all her books and crayons. And she always took her cat Quibbles.

Sometimes when Holly was playing she could hear Mum doing things in the kitchen. Mum often sang or whistled when she was busy. Holly hadn't learned how to whistle yet but, if she knew the words of the song, she sang too. Holly thought being under the table was magic. She called it Holly's World.

One day Holly was having breakfast in the kitchen. It was raining outside and quite windy, but she didn't mind. She had a new toy to play with – Tiny Teddy. He was the smallest teddy in the world. He was so small he could sit in an egg cup. He was sitting in an egg cup now watching Holly eat her breakfast. Holly couldn't wait to show him Holly's World.

It was very quiet in the kitchen. Mum was busy upstairs and the only sounds were the rain on the window and crunch, crunch as Holly ate her toast. Even Quibbles the cat was quiet. Holly could hear him snoring softly under the table. Then someone started singing. It was a song Holly had never heard before.

"I'm a hippso-piti-potimus,
I'm very small and sweet.
I'm lonely playing on my own,
I wish that we could meet."

"It must be Mum," Holly said to Tiny Teddy. Tiny Teddy looked at her with his tiny black button eyes.

The singing started again.

"I'm a hippso-piti-potimus,
I'm very small and sweet.
I'm lonely playing on my own,
I wish that we could meet."

It didn't sound like Mum's voice. And it didn't seem to be coming from upstairs. It sounded as if it was coming from under the kitchen table, from Holly's World.

Holly lifted the tablecloth and looked underneath. She couldn't see anything unusual. There were the books and pencils she had been using yesterday. There was her doll Rosemary. There was Corkscrew the clown, looking fed up because he had been under the table all night. There was Quibbles the cat, asleep on the rug. Everything looked the same as it always did.

Then Holly heard a shuffling sound coming from behind a big, red cushion. All of a sudden a funny face peeped round.

"Hello," said the face, shyly.

"Hello," said Holly, surprised.

"I'm Albert," said the face.

"I'm Holly," said Holly.

There was a pause.

"I'm a hippso-piti-potimus," said Albert.

"I've never seen a hippso-piti-potimus before," said Holly.

Albert lowered his eyes. Holly noticed he had long eyelashes.

"Will you sing your song again?" she asked.

Albert started to sing.

"I'm a hippso-piti-potimus,
I'm very small and sweet.
I'm lonely playing on my own,
I wish that we could meet."

"I'd like to play with you," said Holly.

The Hippso-piti-potimus smiled. He had a lovely smile. It spread across his face.

"Come and play at my house," he said. "You'll really like it. There's a river, and trees, and red and yellow birds that talk."

"Parrots!" cried Holly.

"Yes," said Albert, "and big grey things that walk in a line holding on to each other."

"Elephants!" said Holly, clapping her hands together.

"And orangey things that roar."

"Lions!"

"And swinging things in trees, and curled up hissing things. And hanging things..." Albert went on, talking quickly.

Holly laughed. "When can we go?"

"Now, if you like," said Albert.

"Can I bring Tiny Teddy?" asked Holly.

Albert nodded. "Shut your eyes and give me your hand," he said.

Holly put Tiny Teddy in her pocket and held out her hand. Albert touched it with his cold wet nose. Holly heard a rushing sound and felt a soft breeze on her face.

When she opened her eyes everything was different. She was in a warm, sunny place. In front of her was a bluey-green river, and behind her were lots of tall trees. Somewhere, far away, she heard the roar of a lion. Monkeys were swinging through the trees, whooping and yelling with excitement. At the edge of the river two baby elephants were about to wade into the water. One was holding the tail of the other with his trunk.

When the elephants saw Holly they stopped playing.

"Who are you?" asked one.

"Holly," replied Holly.

"What's a Holly?" asked the other.

"I'm a girl," said Holly.

The two elephants looked at each other and started to laugh.

"What's so funny?" asked Holly, smiling. But the elephants were laughing so much they could not speak.

"Take no notice of them," said Albert. "They laugh all the time."

"Can girls do this?" asked one of the

elephants, and he sucked up some water with the tip of his trunk and then squirted it up in the air.

"I haven't got a trunk," said Holly.

"Why not?" asked one of the elephants.

"Because I don't need one," said Holly.

"How do you eat, then?"

"With a knife and fork," said Holly. This made the elephants laugh again.

"How do you squirt water?" they asked.

"I don't," said Holly. This time the baby elephants looked amazed.

"Then how do you get washed?" they asked.

"I have a bath," said Holly. "With bubbles in it," she added.

"Oh, lucky thing," said the elephants, "we like bubbles."

"I'll bring some next time," promised Holly.

"Girls are different from us," said

Albert. "Girls use bubble bath, and wear clothes and go to school. Girls stand on two feet and do everything with their hands."

"Show us," said the elephants.

Holly undid the ribbon in her hair and did it up again.

"I bet Monkey could do that," said one of the elephants. "He's got hands."

"He can pick his nose," said the other elephant.

"It's rude to pick your nose," said Holly.

There was a whooshing sound as Monkey swung down from the high branch of a tree to the ground. "Did someone mention my name?" he asked.

"Show Holly your hands," said one elephant.

Monkey held out one hand. It was exactly the same as hers. Holly and Monkey linked their little fingers. "Now we are friends," said Holly.

The others wanted to link little fingers too. But they didn't have any fingers, so they linked tails instead.

"Now come and meet Lion Cub," said Albert.

Holly loved Lion Cub. He liked to be tickled under the chin, just like Quibbles.

"Watch his sharp claws," said Albert. But when he played, Lion Cub kept his claws tucked away between his toes.

"Quibbles does that as well," Holly told him.

"Who's Quibbles?" asked Lion Cub.

"He's my cat," said Holly.

After she had played with Lion Cub, Holly met Albert's mum and dad and all his brothers and sisters. Mrs Hippso-piti-potimus made a special tea for her. There were pineapple chunks and little cubes of cheese, and triangles of pizza with salad and fresh crusty bread. In a big dish in the

middle of the
table was a
red wobbly
jelly and
milky-white
ice cream
with frozen
chocolate
on the top.
And in tall
glasses were
milkshakes
made from
whipped-up fruits
of the forest.

"Albert told me what
little girls like to eat," Mrs Hippso-piti-
potimus told Holly.

After tea they walked down to the
water's edge and Albert showed her how he
could keep his head underwater for ages

and ages. Holly felt sad when it was time to go home.

"Come again soon," said Mr and Mrs Hippso-piti-potimus.

"Come again soon," said Monkey and Lion Cub.

"Come again soon," said the two baby elephants.

"I will, I will," said Holly, kissing them all.

"Next time you come you will see Bronti-sori-sorus," said Albert. "He can't wait to show you his shell collection." Then bending forward, Albert touched Holly's hand with his cold nose.

The next thing Holly heard was Mum's voice calling her name. She opened her eyes. She was under the kitchen table. Sitting next to her were Rosemary and Corkscrew, and on her lap was Quibbles the cat.

"There you are," said Mum, peering under the table. "I've been looking for you."

"I've been playing with Albert," yawned Holly.

"Who's Albert?" asked Mum.

Holly told Mum about Albert and Monkey and Lion Cub, and about the two baby elephants. She told her about the special tea that Mrs Hippso-piti-potimus had made for her. "And next time I'm going to meet Bronti-sori-sorus," she said.

Mum listened carefully. Then she took Holly on her lap.

"Holly," she said, "there aren't any Brontosauruses left in the world. They all died a long time ago."

"This is a Bronti-sori-sorus," said Holly, "and he's going to show me his shells. Albert said some of them are as big as dinner plates." She got off Mum's lap and started to sing.

"I'm a hippso-piti-potimus,
I'm very small and sweet.
I'm lonely playing on my own,
I wish that we could meet."

"What a lovely song!" said Mum.

"It's Albert's song," said Holly. "Next time he comes you can meet him."

But Albert didn't come again. Holly listened for his song every day. But she didn't hear it. She sometimes wondered if she had ever really seen him. Perhaps she had dreamed the whole thing. She stopped playing in Holly's World. It didn't seem like a magical place any more.

Then one day Holly's friend Tabitha came to play and asked to see Tiny Teddy. Holly couldn't find him anywhere. She looked in all the egg cups in case he was curled up asleep. She emptied her toy cupboard. She looked under her bed. Then, she remembered she had taken him with her when she went to play with Albert. She had put him in her skirt pocket.

"Mum," she called, rushing downstairs, "did you see Tiny Teddy in my skirt pocket?"

"No," said Mum, "I haven't seen Tiny Teddy for ages."

Holly looked as if she might cry. "Don't

worry," said Mum, "he's hiding somewhere, and he is so small you can't see him. He'll turn up." But Holly didn't think he would.

About a week later, Holly was sitting in the kitchen when she heard the sound of someone singing. The song was very faint and then it stopped. Holly held her breath, hoping she would hear it again. But the only sounds were the clock ticking and Quibbles purring on her lap.

Then it started again. This time it was louder. It was coming from under the table.

"I'm a bronti-sori-sorus,
I'm feeling sad and blue.
All my friends have gone away,
I'd like to play with you!"

When Holly lifted the tablecloth, she

came face to face with the silliest-looking creature she had ever seen.

His huge body filled up all the space, and his small head was flattened against the top of the table. He gave Holly a big lopsided grin.

"Are you Holly?" he asked.

"Yes," said Holly. "Are you...Bronti-sori-sorus?"

The silly-looking creature nodded. "I'm Bruno," he said.

"Why didn't Albert come?" asked Holly. "I wanted to see him."

"He wanted to see you, too," said Bruno, " but he's got measles. He asked me to give you this."

Then Bruno held out an egg cup. Sitting in it, looking at Holly with his tiny bright black eyes, was Tiny Teddy.

"So it wasn't a dream after all," said Holly, stroking Tiny Teddy's head with her little finger.

"Come back with me now and see my shell collection," suggested Bruno.

Holly thought for a minute. Perhaps she would go, just for a while. It would be nice to play with Albert, and see Lion Cub and Monkey and all the others.

But this time she wouldn't take Tiny Teddy with her. After all, she didn't want to leave him behind...again!

Billy Bear's Big Day

Billy Bear was feeling very happy as he skipped along the woodland path.

He was going to meet his best friends, Sammy Squirrel, Freddy Fox and Ronald Rabbit. They were going to play hide-and-seek in the woods all afternoon. Billy Bear loved hide-and-seek. It was his favourite game in the whole world.

"I'll make sure they can't find me when it's my turn to hide," thought Billy, munching on a delicious juicy apple.

Billy and his friends had agreed to meet by the big oak tree in the middle of the woods.

When he got there, his friends hadn't arrived, so he sat under the tree to enjoy the rest of his apple.

"Mmm…delicious," he said, licking the last of the juicy apple from his fingers. When he'd finished, his friends still hadn't arrived.

"Oh dear," thought Billy. "If they don't come soon, I might fall fast asleep. I feel very comfortable sitting here."

His eyes started to close. His head started to droop, and moments later Billy was fast asleep.

The next thing he heard was Ronald Rabbit shouting in his ear, "Wake up, Billy!"

Billy slowly opened his eyes, and saw Sammy Squirrel, Freddy Fox and Ronald Rabbit all looking down at him.

"Hello everyone!" said Billy, pleased to see his friends. "I must have fallen asleep. Have you been here long?"

"We've only just arrived," said Freddy

Fox.

"I'm really looking forward to playing hide-and-seek," said Ronald Rabbit excitedly. "Are we all ready?"

"I'm ready," said Billy Bear, standing up.

"I'm ready too," said Freddy Fox.

"And me," said Sammy Squirrel.

They decided that Ronald Rabbit should go first. They all shut their eyes and counted to ten while Ronald ran off to hide.

"One, two, three, four, five, six, seven, eight, nine, TEN! Coming, ready or not!"

they all yelled.

Sammy Squirrel looked inside a prickly bush…but Ronald wasn't hiding there.

Freddy Fox looked behind a mossy bank…but Ronald wasn't hiding there either.

"I wonder where he is?" asked Billy, looking up at a tall tree.

Suddenly, he spotted Ronald hiding up among the branches.

"I can see him! I can see him!" yelled Billy to the others.

"Well done, Billy. You've found me," said Ronald, racing back down to the ground. Now you run and hide, while we shut our eyes and count to ten."

Billy ran off into the woods as fast as his legs could carry him.

"Where can I hide?" thought Billy, as

he hurried along. "I know! I'll hide in the river." But the river looked far too cold to hide in. "I'll hide up a tree like Ronald did!" But then he remembered that bears aren't very good at climbing trees.

"Coming, ready or not!"

he heard the others shout.

"Oh no…they're coming. And I haven't found anywhere to hide yet!" thought Billy.

Suddenly, he saw a big pile of leaves in front of him.

"I'll hide under these leaves. They'll never find me here," he thought excitedly.

Billy lay down as quickly as he could, then used his paws to rake all the leaves over him until he was completely hidden.

"This is a really good hiding place," he thought, giggling to himself.

Billy could hear his friends looking for him.

"Come out, Billy," they called. "Come out, come out, wherever you are."

Their voices got louder as they got closer to him. Billy held his breath as his three friends almost walked right over him. He lay as still as he could so he wouldn't give himself away. Soon, the voices grew quieter as his friends searched in another part of the wood.

"Hee, hee…I've fooled them all," chuckled Billy.

He listened for a long time until the voices faded away.

"They're a long way away. They won't find me now," he thought.

But after a little while, Billy started to get hungry. And it was very boring lying under a pile of leaves with nothing to do.

Billy grew hungrier and hungrier. And a strange growling noise started to come from his tummy.

"Oh, no," he thought. "I must be really hungry. My tummy's starting to rumble!"

Just then, Billy heard another noise. It was a funny, buzzing noise.

"I wonder what that is?" he thought.

He carefully brushed the leaves away from his eyes, and saw a bee flying around a flower nearby.

"A bee!" cried Billy. "Where there's a bee, there's usually my favourite food...honey. If I follow it, the bee might lead me to some."

Slowly, Billy crawled out from under the leaves so he wouldn't annoy the bee. Then he hid behind a bush and waited for it to fly off.

"Rumble...rumble!" went Billy's tummy.

"Sshh!" whispered Billy, looking down at his tummy. "You'll frighten the bee away

if you make so much noise."

Luckily, the bee didn't hear Billy's tummy rumble. It just hopped from one flower to another flower.

Billy followed a little way behind. Every time the bee stopped to buzz around a flower, Billy hid behind a bush or a tree.

"This is like playing hide-and-seek with a bee!" Billy laughed to himself.

Sometimes, the bee flew away so fast, it was difficult for Billy to keep up with it.

"Whoa…slow down," he puffed, running as fast as he could.

Billy followed the bee deeper and deeper into the woods. Finally, it flew up into a tall tree. Billy looked up and saw a large honeycomb in the branches.

"Hooray!" he yelled. "A honeycomb! And inside it will be lots of scrumptious honey."

The bee buzzed around the honeycomb for a while, and then flew quickly off.

Billy stood on tiptoe, stretched up and put his paw inside the honeycomb. When he took it out, it was covered in delicious, sticky honey.

"Yummy!" he said, licking the honey off his paw.

Billy put his paw back into the honeycomb and licked it again and again, until there was no more honey left.

Billy's tummy was so full of honey he could hardly walk. He leaned against the tree and didn't move. He felt *so* tired!

"I've had a really BIG day today," he yawned. "First, I had a really BIG game of hide-and-seek. Then, I had a really BIG adventure chasing the bee through the woods. Then I had a really BIG meal of honey. No wonder I feel so tired."

Billy leaned his head back against the tree, and soon he was fast asleep.

Some time later, Billy woke up to the sound of buzzing in his ears.

"I wonder what that is?" he thought, rubbing his eyes. When he opened them he saw a whole swarm of bees buzzing angrily around his head.

"Oh, no!" yelled Billy. "They must be annoyed with me for eating all their honey."

He leaped up and began to walk quickly along the woodland path.

Billy looked over his shoulder, and to his horror he saw that the angry swarm of bees was following him.

He began to walk faster. But the faster he moved, the faster the bees flew after him.

Billy started to run as fast as he could. But the bees flew a lot faster and they were catching up with him…fast!

"What am I going to do?" he thought, nervously. "If I don't get away from them, they'll catch me up and sting me all over!"

Billy looked around, but he couldn't see anywhere to hide.

The bees had almost caught up with

him, when out of the corner of his eye Billy noticed a small pond.

"Bees hate water," he suddenly remembered.

He ran to the pond and jumped straight in.

The bees stopped at the pond's edge. They flew around angrily for a little while, then with one loud **"Buzzzzzz!"** they flew back into the woods.

Billy struggled out of the pond and sat down on the ground. He was very wet, and he began to shiver with the cold. He looked around and r e a l i z e d that he'd never

been to this part of the woods before. He was completely lost.

"What a silly bear I am," he thought sadly. "If I hadn't been so greedy for honey, I wouldn't be sitting here now – wet, cold and lost."

Billy began to feel scared. He'd never been lost before.

Suddenly, he remembered the special rhyme his mother had taught him:

"If you are lost,
and there's no one around,
stay where you are,
until you are found."

"I'll just stay right here," thought Billy. "My friends are sure to find me soon."

As time went on, it began to grow darker. Billy started to feel even more scared.

"Help!" he shouted. "I'm over here! Can anyone hear me?"

He listened for an answer. But the only thing Billy could hear was the wind whistling through the branches of the trees.

Suddenly, he heard a loud hooting noise.

"Who's there?" he asked in a shaky voice.

"Toowhit, toowoo!" It was only a large owl, perched high up in a tree.

Then Billy heard another noise. It sounded like voices, but they were coming from a long way away.

Billy listened as hard as he could.

"Billy! Billy! Where are you?" the voices called.

Billy realized it was his three friends!

"I'm over here!" he yelled back excitedly.

The voices came nearer and nearer. Suddenly, out of a small clearing popped Sammy Squirrel, Freddy Fox and Ronald Rabbit.

"Thank goodness you've found me," said Billy. "I was getting really scared out here all by myself."

"We've been looking for you all afternoon," said Freddy Fox. "We were getting very worried. Where have you been?"

When Billy told them of his adventure with the bees, they all agreed that he had been a very silly Billy, indeed.

"I'm sorry for making you so worried," said Billy in a little voice. "I promise I'll never be so silly again."

"Never mind, Billy," said Ronald

Rabbit. "We're all a bit silly sometimes. We're just glad to find you safe and sound."

Slowly, Ronald brought out a great big jar of honey from behind his back.

"Here you are, Billy. We thought you might need cheering up."

"Oh, thank you!" said Billy gratefully. "What kind friends you are!"

He took the top off the jar, put in his paw and scooped out a great big pile of sticky honey.

"What a lucky bear I am," thought Billy. "Two lots of delicious honey in one day…yummy!"

The Magic Boots

Daniel was bored. He had eaten his snacks. He had read his book and even done all the puzzles in his puzzle pad. He looked out of the car window, and counted the cows. Then he counted the sheep.

"My legs have gone stiff," he complained. "Are we nearly there yet?"

"Wiggle your toes," suggested Mum, looking over her shoulder. "It won't be long now. Pirate Cove is just over this hill."

"First one to see the sea!" said Daniel, wiggling his toes. He leaned forwards and looked out of the car window again. "There it is!"

He pointed excitedly. As they came

over the hill, they could see the small village of Pirate Cove. The sea sparkled in the evening sun, as they drove down the twisting road into the village.

"Here we are…at last," said Mum. They drove through two large open gates and up a long lane towards Grandma's house.

Bumpety, bumpety, bump!

Mum's car bounced as they drove along the lane. Daniel held on tight.

"There's Grandma," said Mum, as they reached the top of the hill. Daniel opened his window and waved.

"Hello Grandma!" he yelled. "I've come to stay!"

Grandma waved back. "Welcome to Pirate Cove," she called, rushing to give him a great big granny hug. "And welcome to my house, too."

"I'm staying with you for a whole night," Daniel said proudly. "All on my own!"

"I'll be back tomorrow afternoon to pick you up," said Mum. "I hope you'll be a good boy."

"But not TOO good, Daniel," added Grandma, winking. Daniel, Mum and Grandma walked up to the house together. As they walked, Daniel breathed in big deep breaths. The air smelled funny – like fish and salt and seaweed all mixed up together – but he liked it. It made him feel happy.

"Can I see Bluebeard?" he asked, as they went inside the house. Bluebeard was Grandma's parrot. He was very old. A long time ago he had belonged to a great uncle, but now he belonged to Grandma.

"Of course," replied Grandma. "Give him a nut! They're his favourite."

Daniel opened the sitting-room door and went in. Bluebeard was snoozing on his perch, but he soon woke up.

"Pieces of eight! Pieces of eight!" squawked the bird, when Daniel offered him a nut.

"What are pieces of eight?" asked Daniel. "Parrot food?"

"Oh no!" chuckled Grandma. "That's what pirates called their gold." She winked at Daniel. "The silly old bird thinks he's a pirate!"

Daniel unpacked his things. Then they all had a drink and a biscuit. Before long, it was time for Mum to leave, and for Daniel to get ready for bed.

"Have fun!" said Mum, giving him a big squeeze. "I'll be back tomorrow."

The moon was shining brightly as Grandma helped Daniel get into his pyjamas. It made strange shadows on the bedroom wall.

"Look at the sea, Grandma!" whispered Daniel, pulling back the curtain and peeping out. The water was twinkling, as if it was full of stars. "It's like magic!"

Grandma nodded. "Maybe it is magic," she replied. "Anything can happen at Pirate Cove, you know!"

"What do you mean?" asked Daniel, hopping into bed. "What kind of things?"

"Oh, magical things," said Grandma. "It's that kind of place. Now snuggle down. If the weather is fine in the morning, we'll go and explore the pirates' caves in the cove. They say treasure was buried there."

Daniel closed his eyes, and listened to

the swish of the waves on the shore. Soon he was fast asleep, dreaming of pirate treasure.

The next morning, the sky was full of big black clouds and it was raining hard.

"Don't worry, Daniel," said Grandma, clearing away the breakfast things. "I'm sure the sun will come out this afternoon. Then we can go to the caves."

Daniel cheered up. "Can I play with Bluebeard this morning?" he asked.

Grandma's eyes twinkled. "Of course," she smiled. "Why don't you and Bluebeard explore the house while I finish some jobs. He'll show you around."

"Oh, yes please!" cried Daniel. "I love exploring. Let's go, Bluebeard!"

The parrot spread his wings and flew off through the kitchen door.

"Wait for me!" called Daniel, as the bird swooped along the hallway and up the stairs.

"Pieces of eight!" squawked the noisy parrot. He sailed along the landing and landed on top of a big vase by a door.

Daniel tried to open the door. It wouldn't move.

"We can't go in there," he told Bluebeard. "It's locked."

The parrot gave a loud shriek. Then he poked his head in the vase, and pulled out a rusty key.

"Wow!" cried Daniel. Carefully, he tried the key in the lock. It turned easily. Very slowly, he opened the door and stepped inside. Ahead, there was a steep, dark staircase. Before Daniel could say a word, Bluebeard flew off the vase and swooped up the stairs.

"Wait for me!" cried Daniel.

"GOSH!" was all he could say when he reached the top of the stairs. He was in the attic. He stared around the room, mouth wide open. Cardboard boxes and suitcases lay all about, and there were old pictures and dusty furniture piled up against the walls. Everything was covered in thick cobwebs.

Daniel looked for Bluebeard. He was perched on top of a huge black chest in the corner, looking extremely pleased with himself. The chest was very old. It was

covered in dents and scratches, and had thick bands of gold wrapped around it.

"Perhaps it's a treasure chest," whispered Daniel, going over to look at it more closely. His heart pounded as he lifted the lid. Maybe there would be treasure inside.

"OH!" he cried. "It's full of clothes."

Daniel pulled out old hats and dresses. Suddenly he spotted something shining at the bottom.

"What's that?" he wondered. "It looks like a buckle." Daniel tugged hard and pulled out a pair of big black leather boots. Each boot had a golden buckle on the side.

"They look like a pirate captain's boots!" laughed Daniel. He put them on and marched up and down the attic, trying his best to be a fierce pirate. "Shiver my timbers!" he roared. "Come on, Bluebeard! Let's go and show Grandma."

Clomp! Clomp! Clomp!

Daniel thumped down the attic stairs in the big black boots. Bluebeard perched on his shoulder.

"I wish I really was a pirate captain," said Daniel, opening the door at the bottom. "Then we could find some real treasure."

Just at the very moment when Daniel made his wish, something strange happened – something *very* strange indeed. Instead of stepping through the door onto Grandma's landing, Daniel stepped out onto the deck of a ship. It was a huge *pirate* ship that was far out at sea.

"Where are we?" cried Daniel, looking around in amazement. "How did we get here?"

He looked down at the boots. Then he looked at Bluebeard.

"They must be magic," he whispered. "Grandma did say magical things happen here!"

Just then, a voice called from above. "Ahoy there, Capt'n!"

Daniel looked up, and felt very dizzy. High above, up in the ship's rigging, was a pirate. He was looking out to sea through a telescope.

"Land ahoy, Capt'n!" yelled the pirate, pointing to a small island.

Daniel looked around. There was no one else on deck.

"Is he talking to me?" he asked Bluebeard. "I'm not the captain!"

Step! Clump! Step!

Clump! Step! Clump!

Daniel heard footsteps. Three huge pirates appeared on the ship's deck. One pirate had a wooden leg, one had a hook

instead of his right hand, and one wore a large black eye patch.

"Aye, aye, Capt'n," growled the three pirates, grinning at Daniel. He grinned back. "They all think I'm the ship's captain," he thought, chuckling. "It must be the magic."

Daniel was starting to enjoy himself. "Come on, Bluebeard," he whispered. "Let's have some fun."

"Drop anchor and hoist the Jolly Roger flag, men!" ordered Daniel. "We're going to row ashore and dig for treasure!"

"Hooray!" cheered the ship's crew. "Three cheers for the Capt'n."

The ship's crew lowered a boat over the side, and everyone climbed aboard – except for Bluebeard, who flew instead.

"YO HO HO!" roared the pirates, as they rowed for the shore. "We're going to be rich!"

Daniel counted the crew ashore. "One, two, three, four, five...good," he said. "Now for the treasure!"

The crew crowded around Daniel, waiting for their next orders.

"Where do we dig, Capt'n?" asked the ship's first mate. "Show us the map."

"What map?" asked Daniel.

"The treasure map, of course, Capt'n,"

growled one of the pirates. "You can't find treasure without a treasure map!"

Daniel began to feel worried. He had been so excited about digging for treasure that he hadn't stopped to think about where to find it.

"You do have a map, don't you?" asked one of the pirates. He looked a bit angry.

"Well, um, no," admitted Daniel, taking a step back. "I don't, actually."

Suddenly there was a loud squawk. Bluebeard swooped down and landed on Daniel's shoulder.

"What am I going to do, Bluebeard?" whispered Daniel. "These pirates want their treasure...and they want it now!"

"Shiver my timbers!" cried the noisy bird. Then he flew off.

The crew watched as Bluebeard swooped across the beach and landed on a rock next to a palm tree.

"Pieces of eight! Pieces of eight!" squawked Bluebeard. He did a funny little dance and flapped his wings excitedly.

"What's that stupid bird up to?" growled one of the pirates. "I wish he'd be quiet!"

"Perhaps he's trying to tell us something," thought Daniel. "He's very excited about something."

All of a sudden, Daniel began to jump about too. "That's it!" he cried. "Pieces of eight means pirate gold! Grandma said so! Clever Bluebeard! He's showing us where the treasure is buried. Let's get to work!"

DIG! DIG! DIG! CLUNK!

It wasn't long before the pirates' shovels hit something hard. It was a big chest, buried in the sand.

"Well done, men!" cried Daniel, as the pirate crew lifted the chest out onto the beach. "Let's open it!"

CREEEEAK!

Daniel and the crew opened the lid of the chest.

"Hooray!" they cheered. Hundreds of gold coins showered onto the sand.

Bluebeard landed on the lid of the chest. "Pieces of eight! Pieces of eight!" he shrieked, picking up a gold coin in his beak.

"YO HO HO!" roared the pirates,

dancing a jig on the beach. "We're rich! Three cheers for Bluebeard and the Capt'n."

On Daniel's orders, the pirates carried the chest to the boat. Then they rowed back to the ship.

"Follow me, men!" cried Daniel, when everyone was back on board. "We'll share out the treasure in my cabin."

Daniel opened the door of the captain's cabin and stepped inside. He rubbed his eyes and blinked. Then he blinked again. The treasure chest had disappeared. The crew had disappeared. Even the pirate ship had disappeared. He was back on Grandma's landing!

"Pieces of eight! Pieces of eight!" squawked Bluebeard, landing on Daniel's shoulder.

Daniel chuckled. "At least you're still here," he said, stroking the parrot's head.

"Let's go and find Grandma. She'll NEVER believe what's happened!"

But Daniel was wrong. Grandma did believe him. She listened very carefully as Daniel told her about his adventure.

"I told you Pirate Cove is a magical place," she smiled, her eyes twinkling. "Those boots belonged to your great uncle. He was a ship's captain, but some people think he was really a pirate! Bluebeard was his parrot once, you know."

Daniel gasped. "So these *are* pirate boots after all. And Bluebeard was a pirate's parrot. That's how he knew where to find the treasure!"

"Pieces of eight! Pieces of eight!" squawked Bluebeard, as if to agree.

"But how did we end up on a pirate ship?" asked Daniel.

"Ah, well, that was magic!" said Grandma wisely. "And it's best not to try and explain magic. You just have to let it happen!"

Milly's
Secret

M illy wanted a puppy. She didn't care how big or small it was. She didn't mind if it was scruffy or well groomed. It didn't even matter if it was naughty! She just wanted her very own puppy to love.

"PLEEEASE can I have a puppy?" begged Milly for the hundredth time. "It's my birthday next week. I PROMISE I'll look after it."

Dad looked up from his newspaper. "You don't even look after your toys!" he said. "You can't play with a puppy just when you feel like it. They need love and care all the time."

"I know, Dad," replied Milly. "Mrs

Jenkins from the kennels told me. You have to feed them, brush them, take them for a walk every day..."

"...and clean up their mess!" sniggered her big brother Jack, holding his nose. "YUCK!"

"But I don't mind!" cried Milly, crossly. "I'd do anything for my puppy!"

Mum ruffled Milly's hair. "Don't get upset," she soothed. "Let's just wait and see, shall we?"

"That's what you always say," sighed Milly. She picked up her drawing pad and stomped out into the garden. "I'm going to do some pictures."

Milly sat down in her favourite corner of the garden and began to draw – a puppy, of course. Her pad was full of them. Fat puppies, thin puppies, fluffy puppies, spotty puppies, pretty puppies, funny puppies. But one thing was the same about all the pictures. Underneath, in her best writing, Milly always wrote the name 'Pip'. That was the name Milly had decided to call her puppy – when she finally got one, of course.

"Don't worry, Pip," said Milly, colouring in her newest picture. "I'll find you one day."

Suddenly, Milly heard a strange sound coming from behind the garden fence. It was a funny, whining kind of noise, and it sounded very sad. Milly put down her pad and peered through a hole in the fence. She could just see a small scared-looking animal huddled in the long grass.

"Poor little thing," said Milly, pushing back a broken fence panel to get a better look. Hearing her kind voice, the furry bundle crept closer. Milly could not believe her eyes.

"It's a puppy!" she whispered in

amazement, scooping
up the scruffy ball
of fur. "He must
be lost."

The puppy
wriggled happily
in Milly's arms,
and looked up
at her with big
brown eyes. His
floppy ears were
tatty-looking and he
had a patch over one eye,
which made him look a bit lopsided. And
as for his coat – it was so matted with mud
that Milly could hardly tell what colour it
was. Milly thought he was perfect!

"You look just like a Pip to me," she
laughed, tickling the puppy's tummy. The
puppy licked her hand, and snuggled in.

Milly sighed a big sigh. "I wish you

were mine, Pip," she said, stroking the puppy's head. "But Mum and Dad will never let me keep you."

Then she had an idea. "Why don't I pretend you're mine, just for the day?" she cried. "You can be my secret puppy!"

As if in reply, the puppy licked her hand again and gave a loud bark.

"SSHH!" whispered Milly, tucking Pip inside her coat. "Someone might hear you! Don't forget, you're a secret!"

Milly crept up the garden path, and looked in at the kitchen window. Mum and Dad were busy doing the washing up, and Jack was sitting in front of the computer as usual. The coast was clear!

As quietly as she could, Milly crept in through the back door and up the stairs to her bedroom. She had just shut the door, and put Pip down on the bed when she heard Dad calling.

"Milly!" he shouted. "Come and help clear up these toys!"

"But Dad..." began Milly.

"No buts," called Dad. "It's time to tidy up!"

Milly quickly made Pip a bed out of an old jumper and pushed it under her own bed. "Stay, boy!" she whispered, helping him snuggle down. "I won't be long!" Then she shut the door behind her and ran downstairs.

It wasn't long before the noises started. Scratch! Scratch! Scratch! At first they were very quiet, so only Milly could hear. But then the noises got louder.

SCRATCH! SCRATCH!

Jack looked up from the computer. "What's that noise?" he asked, staring at Milly.

Milly went red. "What noise?" she replied.

THUD! BANG! CRASH!

"OH NO!" cried Milly, dropping everything and heading up the stairs. Jack was not far behind.

Milly opened her bedroom door and gasped. There was Pip, sitting in the middle of the floor, surrounded by a jumble of books and toys.

"Oh Pip!" exclaimed Milly, picking up the naughty little puppy. "What a mess!"

"Where did he come from?" asked Jack, peering round the door.

"He's my secret puppy!" cried Milly, pulling Jack into the room. "Please don't tell. I'm only keeping him for the day!"

"He won't stay secret for long if he keeps on making a noise like that!" grinned Jack. "It's a good job Mum and Dad are in the garden."

Milly's eyes filled with tears. "It's not his fault," she mumbled. "He was bored up here on his own."

Jack looked at Milly,
then at Pip.
"Don't worry!"
he said. "I'll
help you look
after him. It
will be easier
with two
of us!"

Milly
and Jack
cleared up the
mess together,
while Pip sniffed
happily around the bedroom. Then Jack
looked through one of the pile of books
about dog care in Milly's bookcase.

"Let's make a list of everything we
need to look after a puppy," he said.

They were just searching for some toys

for Pip to play with when they heard footsteps on the landing. Quick as a flash, Jack hid Pip under Milly's dressing gown.

"What are you two up to?' asked Mum, poking her head round the door. "You're very quiet!" Before they could reply, she sniffed the air and pulled a funny face. "What's that smell?" she asked, looking about. "It smells rather...umm...doggy!"

"It might be my football things," said Jack innocently. "They got a bit wet."

"Really, Jack," frowned Mum. "Put them in the washing machine!"

"It's Pip who needs a wash," said Jack, when Mum had gone. "He does smell!"

"He can't help it!" cried Milly. "It's not his fault that he got lost and covered in mud."

"He still needs a wash," replied Jack. "Mum will soon guess who's hiding in your bedroom if we don't clean him up."

Milly had to agree. "Let's give him a bath," she said. "We can use some bubble bath. That will make him smell better."

Milly held Pip, while Jack ran the water for the puppy's bath.

"Hurry up, Jack," she whispered. "Dad's gone out and Mum is talking to Mrs Jones in the garden. They won't catch us if we hurry."

Jack sat Pip in the basin, while Milly squirted a big blob of bubble bath on his fur, and began to scrub. At first, Pip was very good and stayed quite still. But the more bubbles that Milly made, the more Pip began to fidget. And the more Pip began to fidget, the more the water began to slosh about.

SWOOSH! SPLOOSH!

"Careful!" cried Milly, as Pip began to jump about, chasing the bubbles. SPLASH! A wave of dirty water slopped over the side of the basin, soaking the bathroom floor.

"WOOF! WOOF!" barked the naughty puppy, who was having great fun.

"Catch him!" shouted Milly, as a very wet and bubbly Pip tried to climb out. Too late! Before Jack could grab him, Pip had leapt over the side. The puppy raced madly round the bathroom, shaking water and bubbles everywhere.

"Watch out!" cried Jack, grabbing a towel. A shower of water droplets sprayed the children, as they caught the wriggling Pip and wrapped him in the towel.

Milly and Jack looked at the puppy. Then they looked at the bathroom. Pip was clean and sweet-smelling. But they couldn't say the same for the bathroom. There were puddles of water everywhere, not to mention a trail of dirty footprints all over the floor!

"Mum will go mad if she sees this,"

said Jack. "We'd better clear it up."

So Milly and Jack mopped up, while the puppy, who was worn out after all his fun, snoozed under Milly's bed. Just as Milly was wiping up the last of the puddles, Dad appeared.

"Don't tell me you're cleaning the bathroom!" he laughed, looking amazed.

Milly blushed. "We spilled some water," she mumbled, trying very hard not to lie.

Dad smiled. "Not to worry," he said.

"Come and have your tea. It's on the table."

At the mention of food, Milly and Jack looked at each other guiltily. Poor little Pip! They hadn't given him anything to eat all day.

"We can save him some of our tea," whispered Jack, as they sat down at the table. "He can have it when he wakes up."

"Gosh! You two were hungry!" exclaimed Mum, as she cleared away the plates a little later. "You didn't leave a thing!"

Milly looked at the bag of scraps they were hiding under the table and said nothing. It was all very well having a secret puppy, but it didn't feel quite right if you had to tell lies.

"I think it's time we told Mum and Dad about Pip," said Jack, as they went back upstairs. Milly nodded, and a tear rolled down her cheek. "It's been fun pretending that he's ours," she sniffed. "But I don't think it's right to keep him a secret any more."

"Keep what a secret?" asked Mum, who had followed them upstairs.

Milly took a big deep breath. "Pip!" she said, opening her bedroom door. At the sound of Milly's voice, the puppy trotted out onto the landing. She lifted him up in her arms and turned to face her mum.

"I found him in the field," she explained in a little voice. "I know we can't keep him, but I just wanted to pretend he was mine."

"We were going to tell you!" added Jack. "Honestly!"

For a moment, Mum looked very cross. Then she smiled.

"So that's what you two have been up to all day. I thought you were acting strangely."

Mum leaned forwards and tickled Pip's ears. "Woof!" barked Pip, wagging his stumpy tail and licking Milly's hand.

"It looks like Pip wants to pretend he's yours, too," she said. "But he must belong to somebody. I'll ring Mrs Jenkins at the kennels. She might know if someone has lost a puppy."

Milly and Jack took Pip downstairs to feed him and take him out into the garden, while Mum phoned the kennels. When they came back indoors, Mum and Dad were waiting in the kitchen.

"Have you found Pip's owner?" asked Milly, trying very hard not to cry. Even Jack's eyes looked a bit watery.

"We have found an owner," said Dad, looking serious. "Pip is one of Mrs Jenkins' puppies from the kennels. He went missing two days ago. She's very grateful that you found him, and have looked after him so well."

Milly held Pip very tightly in her arms. "Do you think Mrs Jenkins will mind if we keep him until tomorrow?" she asked quietly. "Pip's tired now."

Mum smiled. "Mrs Jenkins says you can keep him for as long as you like," she said. "She's given him to you."

Milly's heart leapt with excitement. "Can I really keep him?" she gasped, hardly able to believe her ears.

Dad nodded. "We were thinking of getting you a puppy for

your birthday, anyway," he said. "But it looks like you have found one for yourself!"

Milly grinned. "It's been fun having you for a secret puppy," she said, kissing Pip's nose. "But it will be much easier having a puppy that everyone can play with!"

The Forgetful Elephant

Alex looked like any other elephant. But there was one thing that made him very different from the others. Elephants are famous for having long memories, but Alex was forgetful. He wasn't just a little bit forgetful. He forgot everything, all the time!

Alex went to the jungle school with lots of other young animals. But as soon as he learned something new, it would go straight out of his brain. It was as if he had never heard it in the first place.

Alex was not a lazy elephant. He worked hard, but nothing stayed in his brain. Then, at the end of every schoolday, he forgot to take his schoolbag home. His friend Cal Crocodile would usually pick it up and drop it round to his home later. Luckily Cal didn't mind. Alex's teacher Mrs Tiger would shake her head every time Alex forgot something.

"Oh dear! Your mind is full of holes, Alex. It's like a sieve! It's very unusual for an elephant," she would sigh.

"I'm sorry. I wish I could remember," Alex would sniff unhappily. Nasty Simon Snake would snigger at him from the back of the class.

At home, Alex was no better.

"Can you go and fetch me some melons and honey for dinner?" his mum would ask. Alex would scamper off.

"Melons and honey...I can do that!" he would mutter to himself. Then he would see some ants building a nest, or a bird having a bath in the stream. Alex would sit and watch them for a while. Suddenly, he'd forget what he was supposed to be doing in the first place.

Finally, his mum sent him to Doctor Hippo. The doctor looked inside Alex's ears. He looked into his trunk and shone a torch into each eye. He said "Hmm!" and "Hah!" several times and scratched his chin. Then he turned to Alex's mum.

"Your son seems to be a very healthy young elephant," said Doctor Hippo. "There are no twigs stuck up his trunk, and no mudpats in his ears."

"But what about his forgetfulness?" asked Alex's mum.

"I have no idea. I have never come across that in an elephant," frowned the doctor. "You could try tying a ribbon around his trunk, I suppose. My hippo grandma used to do that. The ribbon is supposed to remind you that you have to do something important, like taking a mudbath or visiting

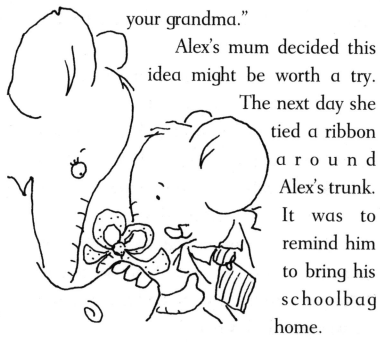

your grandma."

Alex's mum decided this idea might be worth a try. The next day she tied a ribbon a r o u n d Alex's trunk. It was to remind him to bring his s c h o o l b a g home.

But of course, once Alex was out of the house, he forgot all about the ribbon.

"What's that ribbon doing on your trunk?" asked Cal Crocodile.

Alex thought for a moment. He was really puzzled. "That's a good question," he said. "It must be there for a reason."

"Maybe it's there to remind you to do something," suggested Cal.

"That's it! That must be it!" Alex agreed, but then he looked sad. "I can't remember what it was for. I wish I could."

Cal Crocodile had an idea. "My grandma tells me that if you repeat something three times you will remember it forever. You could try it," he suggested.

"OK, I'll give it a go," Alex said. He took a deep breath and began to repeat: "I must remember to take my schoolbag home. I must remember to take my schoolbag home. I must..."

But then a really good game of jungle chase started in the playground. Alex stopped repeating the words so he could join in, and at the end of the schoolday...guess what? Alex forgot his schoolbag.

"Don't give up. Maybe that repeating trick only works for crocodiles, and the ribbon trick only works for hippos," said Cal kindly, when he brought the bag round later. "Perhaps you should ask an elephant grandma what works for elephants."

"Elephants live a long time. I have got a great-great-great grandma called Annie," Alex said proudly. "But I can't remember where she lives."

That evening Alex was playing outside when he heard some jungle birds talking about him in the treetops.

"He gives elephants a bad name. Everyone knows that elephants never forget. He's letting them down," they twittered.

Poor Alex! Tears filled his little elephant eyes. They ran down his cheeks to his little elephant toes.

"I wish I could remember! I wish I could!" he cried, and he ran away into the jungle. He crashed through the bushes crying loudly:

"I wish I could remember!"

He thought he could hear other animals teasing him as he ran.

"There's the silly elephant!" he heard a parrot squawk.

"Silly, silly elephant!" he heard the monkeys chatter.

"You shouldn't be called Alex. You should be called Dumbo!" croaked a jungle frog.

"Or Dozy!" croaked another.

"But I'm not stupid," Alex cried. "It's just that I don't remember things. I wish I wasn't like this," he moaned.

Night began to fall. Very soon, Alex was lost in a part of the jungle he couldn't remember. The farther he ran, the darker the night became. Rain started to pitter-patter around him, and the wind rustled in the trees. Then there was a huge CRASH of thunder, and lightning flashed across the sky over Alex's head.

He began to feel very frightened. He stopped and started to shiver. But then he felt a soft trunk curl around his shoulders. A very old but very kind voice whispered in his ear,

"Hello, Alex. I haven't seen you in a while. You were very small when I saw you last. Haven't you grown?"

Alex turned to see his great-great-great grandma Annie.

"You shouldn't be out here in the

storm," Annie said. "You had better come back to my home. It's just around the corner."

Alex followed Annie through the jungle. As they walked she shaded him from the rain with her big wrinkly ears. Soon they reached a warm dry cave, where Annie sat Alex down. She gave him a big piece of honeycomb to eat.

"Tell me your troubles, little Alex," she smiled. "Elephants don't rush off through the jungle in the dark unless they have troubles."

Alex told her how he couldn't remember things like other elephants. He explained how he wished more than anything in the world that he could change.

"Then I am going to tell you a secret. It's an old elephant secret, but very few elephants remember it, only the very oldest ones," Annie said.

"But I thought elephants remembered everything!" Alex cried.

Annie smiled.

"This secret is so old it takes a lot of remembering, even for an elephant," she said. "Now come with me. You can see this secret with your own eyes."

Alex followed Annie back outside and along a track. Lots of turnings and other paths criss-crossed the track. Each time they reached one of these, Annie stopped and thought hard.

"I am remembering the way," she explained. Alex was pleased that Annie knew where they were going. He had absolutely no idea!

"Here we are," Annie said at last. She stopped in front of a huge jungle tree that seemed to reach up into the sky. It must have been hundreds of years old. It was a huge, wide tree. Annie and Alex walked right around it.

"This is the elephant's wishing tree," Annie explained. "If you want something very very badly, it will help you (if you are an elephant). Now, wish as hard as you can, Alex."

Alex shut his eyes tight. He wished harder than he had ever done in his life.

"I wish I could remember things," he whispered.

"Good. Now, let's get you home," Annie said. They walked back to Annie's cave, where Alex settled down on a pile of warm dry leaves. He fell fast asleep as Annie sang him some very old elephant songs.

When he opened his eyes the next morning Alex felt a little bit confused. Where was he? Then he remembered that he was in great-great-great grandma Annie's cave.

"Hello, Alex. I'm going to take you

home this morning. I got the jungle fireflies to take a message to your mum last night. She knows you're safe but she'll be wanting you back."

Alex started to walk home with Annie,

and as he was walking he noticed a very funny thing. He wasn't forgetting which way to go. He didn't have to look around and think about where he was.

It took a while for Alex to realize that something very important had changed. And then suddenly it struck him.

HE REMEMBERED WHERE HE WAS GOING!

"I can remember just where I live, and where you live, too, Annie!" he shouted out excitedly. "Isn't that fantastic?"

Annie smiled and gave him a cuddle with her trunk.

It took a while to get home because Alex stopped every elephant he saw, and even a monkey and a few parrots.

"Hello, my name is Alex and I can remember how to get home. Isn't that wonderful?" he told them.

When Alex arrived home he couldn't wait to tell everybody the news.

"Something wonderful has just happened to me," Alex said, beaming with joy.

"Well, thank goodness you're home, and you found great-great-great grandma Annie last night!" his mum said. "I was so worried about you! I sent your father out to find you and then all the neighbours and..."

Alex interrupted "I can remember!" he said proudly.

"I didn't get a wink of sleep. It was very naughty to run off like that," Mum carried on.

"Mum! I can remember!" Alex cried.

"What do you mean? What *do* you remember?" asked Alex's dad.

"I remember everything," Alex said.

"EVERYTHING?" Dad laughed. "That's an awful lot to remember. Are you sure about that?"

"I remember Mum's first name, and where I keep my books, and what we all had for dinner last night, and the night before, and the names of all my teachers..." Alex explained.

"What are the names of all your teachers?" Dad asked, testing him out.

"Mrs Tiger, Miss Gorilla, Mr Treesnake and Mrs Hummingbird," replied Alex.

"Very good!" Mum cried.

The whole family was delighted. One by one all the neighbours came over and congratulated Alex. They thought up memory tests for him and he passed every single one. When he went back to school all the other young jungle animals cheered him when he remembered his numbers. Even nasty Simon Snake looked pretty impressed for once.

"Well done, Alex!" Mrs Tiger cried. There were no more problems about Alex remembering his schoolbag either. Every day he took it home, and once he even took Cal's bag home for him when *he* forgot!

Alex's parents threw a special party to tell the good news to the whole jungle.

As the guests were leaving at the end

of the party, Doctor Hippo patted Alex on the back.

"Well, one thing's for sure, Alex, we won't call you the forgetful elephant any more," he said. "But tell me, how were you cured?"

Then Alex remembered something very important his great-great-great grandma Annie had told him.

"The wishing tree is an elephant secret, a very old one that only a few of us know," she had told him. "You must keep the secret, Alex."

Alex had promised that he would.

So when Doctor Hippo asked his question, Alex turned to him and smiled.

"How was I cured of my forgetfulness?" he replied. "Well, do you know something? I really can't remember."

Out of the corner of his eye, Alex saw his great-great-great grandma Annie give him a big wink.

The Dragon's Egg

Wizard Wazoo was in big trouble. In fact, he was in the biggest trouble of his terribly troubled life. Ever since he was a small wizard, he had made mistakes. A mistake in your maths homework can be a problem. It might make your teacher or your parents cross. But Wizard Wazoo's mistakes turned his teacher blue or made his whole house disappear. He seemed to be in trouble more often than he was out of it. And even his cat Carlaminda couldn't help him.

Wizard Wazoo's very bad trouble started because he loved strawberries. Everyone knows that you can only get the best strawberries in summer. But Wizard

Wazoo didn't want to wait until summer to enjoy his favourite fruit. He decided to do a spell. A little bit of wand-waving here, a sprinkling of magic dust there, and hey presto…straw!

"Ooops!" said Wizard Wazoo, staring at the large pile of straw. He bit his wizard lip and muttered his special wizard words: "Da DA!" In a second, the pile of straw turned into a pile of…cranberries.

Cranberries are very tasty indeed. They make a yummy drink. They go well with turkey. But they're no good for a wizard who wants strawberries.

Wizard Wazoo rolled up his sleeves. He cleaned out his spare cauldron and started a strawberry-making spell. He added snails, slug-slime, used teabags, peppermint foot lotion, toenails, cabbage juice and orange peel. It was very smelly.

Wizard Wazoo stirred and tried to

remember the magic words. But he hadn't read the spell very carefully. Carlaminda saw the green steam rising up slowly from the cauldron. She ran under the bed and stayed there with her head in her paws.

Soon, the green steam turned to blue steam. The smell became very bad indeed. The mixture bubbled and popped in a very odd way.

"Let me look in my spell book again," he muttered, as he turned the pages. The ones that he looked at the most were stained red, green and yellow with past spells.

Wizard Wazoo checked his ingredients and read the instructions. And that was when he made his BIG mistake. He turned over two pages at once and did something that no wizard should ever do. He said the magic words backwards: "AD, ad!"

There was a long, long silence. The

only sounds were the bubbling of the mixture and the whimpering of Carlaminda. She had lived with Wizard Wazoo since she was a little kitten. She had a pretty good idea of what was going to happen next.

Suddenly, it was as if three brass bands and a road drill had squeezed into the room at once. Everything that could clatter clattered. Everything that could bong bonged. The glasses tinkled. The windows twinkled (loudly). Wizard Wazoo's teeth chattered. He had a very strange feeling, as if someone was trying to turn him inside out. Then there was a puff of orange smoke and a clash of saucepan lids.

The house zoomed into the air and headed for the very coldest part of Siberia.

The house whirled and whizzed through the sky. Wizard Wazoo shut his eyes until it landed. Then he looked out of the window at the icy land.

"I feel very, very cold," he grumbled to Carlaminda as he shivered and shook. He lit his fire and pulled his cloak around him.

"This is a very big problem," said Wizard Wazoo. "Now I have to work out how to get home."

Worst of all, his wish for strawberries had not gone away. He wanted strawberries more than ever. And if there was one thing that Wizard Wazoo knew about Siberia, it was that strawberries were very hard to find.

The fire was roaring under his spare cauldron. But Wizard Wazoo soon had icicles growing from his toes. It was very hard to concentrate on his spell book when he felt so cold. But he had to find a spell that would take him home.

He looked through all the easy spells at the front of his book, hoping to find something he could use. But none of them said anything about Siberia. Even the quite-hard spells in the middle of the book were no use. Wizard Wazoo hardly ever tried those spells anyway. They were very tricky. But now the freezing wizard had to look at the very difficult spells at the end of the book.

The last part of the book had shiny white pages. They had never been touched by a wizard's fingers. They told Wizard Wazoo about problems that he hadn't even thought of. His eyes opened wider and wider at each page he read.

"How to tame a wild brontosaurus," he read, looking at the three pages of ingredients. "How to take mice out of your ears." (That one sounded very difficult.) "How to make people forget when you've been naughty." That sounded like a useful spell. But it seemed to need wizarding skills that Wizard Wazoo could never learn.

Poor Wizard Wazoo's feet felt like ice. His fingers really were frozen hard by now. He had almost given up hope when he turned the last page. At last, here was the spell he needed. "How to send your house back home from Siberia and find strawberries at the same time."

Wizard Wazoo felt very excited. He read through the list of ingredients.

"Hmm! Now have I got everything I need?" he asked himself. "Fingernail clippings – yes! Marmalade – yes! Cucumber face cream and a pink sponge – yes! Lawnmower oil – yes! Sixteen-day-old pea soup – strangely enough, yes! Two holly leaves – yes! The longest quill of a bad-tempered porcupine – yes! A broken pocket mirror – yes! Three jars of pickled onions – yes, yes, yes! A dragon's egg – oh no, no, no…!" cried Wizard Wazoo.

The dragon's egg was the very last ingredient, and poor Wizard Wazoo knew very well that he didn't have one. He looked around his frosty room, but he knew it was hopeless. Dragons' eggs are big. They are not the kind of thing you could miss. Wizard Wazoo crouched over his fire and tried to think. But it is very hard to think when there are icicles hanging off the ends of your eyelashes.

At that moment, Carlaminda crawled out from under the bed. She felt she couldn't bear to stay in Siberia a moment longer than she had to. She curled around Wizard Wazoo's shivering legs. She pointed her pretty paw at the word 'dragon' and then waved it at the window.

But Wizard Wazoo just stared at her. "What on earth are you trying to tell me, Carlaminda?" he asked.

Carlaminda gave a deep sigh. Sometimes Wizard Wazoo could be very slow. She hurried over to the bookshelf. Then she pulled down a magazine with her teeth and carried it to Wizard Wazoo. He looked down at the brightly coloured cover. It was his favourite magazine – *Magician's Monthly*.

"This is no time to be reading a magazine," he told Carlaminda. But she just pointed her tail at the cover. Wizard

Wazoo read what was written there.

"A new magic cloak in a weekend!

My wife's a witch!

Free with this issue, two packets of super spells!

Siberia: a wonderful land of mystery and magic!"

Wizard Wazoo gasped. There was a picture of a smiling dragon. It was sliding down a snowy slope and waving at the reader with both hands.

Wizard Wazoo peered at the picture. Then he tried to open the magazine to read the story inside. It wasn't easy with frozen fingers, but at last he found the right page. He read that one of the most exciting places in Siberia was the Drooski Dragon Park. Real live dragons could be seen every day. Now, you know that Wizard Wazoo wasn't very clever. But he knew one thing. Where there are dragons, there must also be dragons' eggs.

In no time at all, Wizard Wazoo pulled on his extra-thick woolly socks and wrapped his neck in an old stripy scarf. He pulled his magic wand out of the pot where it had been holding up a plant. He threw open the door, letting in blasts of ice and frozen air. Then he stepped out into the deep snow.

Wizard Wazoo looked right. He looked left. All he could see was shining white snow – everywhere. Then he had an idea. He went back into his house, picked up a wriggling and cross Carlaminda, and tucked her under his cloak. If he was going to find the Drooski Dragon Park, he needed all the help he could get.

The weather outside was truly awful. The snow was whirling around so fast that it made Wizard Wazoo feel dizzy. He got snow in his eyes. He got snow up his nose.

He got snow in his ears and down his extra-thick woolly socks.

"I must keep going!" he said to himself, hunching his shoulders and trying to think himself warmer. He did start to feel a bit warmer. Perhaps his magic was working for once.

The weather started to get better as the wizard walked on through the deep snow. Soon, the snowstorm stopped and the sun came out. It was so bright that it almost blinded Wizard Wazoo. It was hard to know which way to go, but Wizard Wazoo was lucky. He saw a large sign straight ahead:

WELCOME TO THE DROOSKI DRAGON PARK

Entrance charge: 12,000 gold coins

"12,000 gold coins!" gasped Wizard Wazoo. The poor old wizard didn't even have one gold coin, never mind 12,000.

"We'll have to think of something else," he told Carlaminda. He was about to turn back when he noticed something. There was no one at the entrance gate. There was no one to ask for his money! He had happened to turn up just at the moment when the gatekeeper left to eat his lunch.

Wizard Wazoo slipped through the gates and into the park. He picked up a leaflet from an open box as he went past.

Wizard Wazoo had learned his lesson about reading useful instructions. If he had read his spell book properly, he would not have been in Siberia in the first place. So he stopped and read what the leaflet had to say. It told him not to feed the dragons and not to disturb them when they were sleeping. There was also something called: 'Safety note'. It was not very cheerful. It said: 'If you are attacked by a dragon, try screaming. If that doesn't work, you will have nothing more to worry about…ever. Dragons are very fast eaters.'

Wizard Wazoo gulped. "I should have brought my book of spells with me," he moaned. He also thought that maybe mother dragons did not like it when strangers tried to steal their eggs.

Then he had another thought. A dragon's egg might be very heavy, as well as very big. Could he remember enough magic to get it back to his snowy little house?

Wizard Wazoo was not a very good wizard at the best of times. Now he felt as if every simple spell he knew was slipping slowly out of his memory.

"All I need now is to meet an angry dragon and get eaten," he sighed.

"Ahem!" A voice behind him made the wizard spin round. His worst nightmare had come true. Standing in front of him, just six feet away, was the biggest dragon he had ever seen.

Wizard Wazoo had never seen a real dragon before. He had only seen pictures of them in books and magazines. But dragons are much, much bigger in real life. And this dragon didn't just look angry. She looked really furious.

"About time too!" said the dragon. "Come on, come on, let's not hang around here. It's freezing! Are you coming or not?"

Wizard Wazoo looked confused. He thought the dragon was going to eat him. "What?" he asked. "Where?"

"To find an egg, of course," said the dragon crossly. "I don't have any, but my neighbour won't notice if we borrow one."

Wizard Wazoo followed the dragon through the snow. After about ten minutes, they came to a hillside. It was full of big caves. The dragon went into one of the caves. A couple of minutes later, she came out holding something in her scaly arms. It looked like a big grey rock.

Wizard Wazoo almost burst into tears. "I can't carry that!" he cried. "Oh no, whatever am I going to do? I wish I hadn't ever said that spell this morning. Oh dear!"

"Have you quite finished?" asked the

dragon. "I'm going to carry the egg, so stop fussing!"

She bounced off across the snow with the egg, looking back now and then to check that Wizard Wazoo was following her. Inside the wizard's cloak, Carlaminda kept very still. She had a nasty feeling that she might make a tasty snack for a dragon.

They walked past the entrance gate and out of the Drooski Dragon Park. When they reached the wizard's house, they saw that it was almost hidden under the snow.

"This place is too small," sighed the dragon. "Do something about it, will you?"

Wizard Wazoo gaped. "M-m-make it bigger, you mean?" he asked.

"Well, I don't want you to make me smaller," said the dragon, rolling her eyes. "Come on, it's a very easy spell. It's on about page 18 of your spell book, I think."

The wizard rushed into the house and

found his spell book. Then he turned to page 18. He said a few magic words and tapped on the door with his magic wand.

The house gave a loud creak. Then it shook itself and grew to about twice its size. It was still a bit of a squeeze for the dragon to fit through the door, but she got in and dropped the egg on the floor.

"Come on," she said, "get on with the spell, will you? It's too cold to waste time."

"You mean, you're coming, too?" asked Wizard Wazoo.

"Of course," said the dragon.

The wizard tried to imagine the dragon in his quiet little town. It was not easy. He didn't really want a dragon living with him. But he could see there was nothing he could do about it. So he decided to think about the spell instead.

At last all the ingredients were in the cauldron. The only thing left to do was to say the magic words. Wizard Wazoo said them.

There was a loud pop. A breeze of warm air wrapped around the house. There was a shaking and a sound of breaking. Then the house, still much larger, was back in Wizard Wazoo's garden. And there was a large bowl of strawberries on every table. Carlaminda smiled happily and ran outside. The dragon gave a big, toothy smile.

"But why did you help me?" asked the wizard. He gazed at the dragon and reached out for a strawberry.

"For the strawberries of course," she said. "And you can take your hands off that bowl. They're mine!"

What Bigger Bears Are For!

Little Bear was feeling very excited and nervous, all at once. He was going to stay the night with Brown Bear because his mummy was in hospital.

"I've never stayed away from home before," he told Brown Bear. "I feel a bit funny in my tummy."

"Don't worry," said Brown Bear. "I'll look after you. We'll have lots of fun. Why is your mummy in hospital?"

"She's having a baby," replied Little Bear, proudly. "Daddy's going to take me to see them in the morning."

"Why don't we make a card for the baby?" suggested Brown Bear. "You can use my new crayons if you like."

"That's a good idea," smiled Brown Bear's mummy. "There's just enough time to make one before bed."

Mrs Bear fetched some card and scissors. Brown Bear and Little Bear went to find the crayons. Then the two friends stretched out on the floor in Brown Bear's bedroom and began to draw.

"I've done a baby on my card," said Brown Bear.

"And this is a picture of my favourite teddy," squeaked Little Bear. He showed it to his friend.

"What lovely cards!" exclaimed Mrs Bear, coming in to see what they were up to. "It's time to put the crayons away now. You both need a bath before bed."

Mrs Bear let Brown Bear, who was the oldest, turn on the bath taps.

"What can I do?" squeaked Little Bear.

"You can put the bubble bath in," offered Brown Bear. "That's my favourite job!"

"Hurray!" cried Little Bear.

Gloop!

He poured an enormous blob of pink bubble bath into the water. Soon, the bathroom was filled with bubbles!

Splish, splash!

Brown Bear and Little Bear climbed into the bath. It was a bit of a squash, but they didn't mind.

"I play with my sailing boats in the bath at home," said Little Bear.

"You can play with my bath toys," offered Brown Bear. "I've got a big shark, and a whale that squirts water!"

"Oh, thank you, Brown Bear!" cried Little Bear.

The two bears had lots of fun together in the bath.

They played blowing bubbles!

They played shark attack!

They played squirting each other with water!

"What a mess!" laughed Mrs Bear, when it was time to get out. "Did you decide to wash the bathroom too?"

When Brown Bear and Little Bear were dry, they put on their pyjamas.

Little Bear looked down at the buttons on his pyjama top. "It's tricky doing up buttons, isn't it?" he sighed.

"This is how you do it," said Brown Bear, helping Little Bear. "It's easy if you start from the bottom."

"Have you brushed your teeth?" asked Mrs Bear.

"Oops!" laughed Brown Bear. "I forgot. Come on, Little Bear. We've got strawberry toothpaste."

BRUSH! BRUSH! BRUSH!

Brown Bear and Little Bear gave their teeth a good clean.

"That was YUMMY!" giggled Little Bear, as he rinsed out his mouth. "Can we clean them again?"

"Hurry up, you two," smiled Mrs Bear. "It's getting late. It's time for young bears to be in bed."

"Can we have a bedtime story?" asked Little Bear. "I always have a story."

Mrs Bear smiled. "Of course you can, Little Bear," she said. "Brown Bear always has a bedtime story, too. What would you like me to read?"

"Goldilocks and the Three Bears!" shouted Brown Bear and Little Bear together. It was their favourite story ever.

Brown Bear and Little Bear climbed under the covers, while Mrs Bear fetched the book.

"Are you ready?" she asked. Brown Bear and Little Bear nodded. "Then I'll begin. 'Once upon a time, there were three bears...'"

(Of course, Brown Bear and Little Bear knew every word of the story off by heart, as I'm sure you do. So I won't read it all to you now. If you don't know the story, it's about a little girl called Goldilocks. She goes into the Bear family's house when they are out. She eats their porridge. Next she breaks a chair. Then she falls asleep in the baby's bed. But I won't tell you how it ends. Ask someone to read it to you. It's very exciting!)

"Goldilocks was very naughty to go into the bears' house without being invited, wasn't she?" said Brown Bear, when his mummy had finished the story.

"Yes, she was," replied Mrs Bear. "But I don't think she meant to be. She was just being nosy!"

"I hope nobody comes into this house when we're in bed," said Little Bear in a small voice.

"Don't worry, Little Bear!" said Mrs Bear, giving him a squeeze. "Mr Bear and I are downstairs. You're quite safe here!"

"I'll take care of you too," said Brown Bear kindly. "Don't be afraid."

Little Bear smiled a brave smile. "Thank you, Brown Bear," he squeaked.

Mrs Bear shut the bedroom curtains and turned off the light.

"Good night," she whispered, closing the bedroom door. "I'll see you both in the morning."

"Good night, Brown Bear," called Little Bear, snuggling under the covers.

"Good night, Little Bear," replied Brown Bear. "Sleep tight."

Brown Bear pulled the covers up to his ears and shut his eyes. He was just falling asleep when he heard a small voice. It was Little Bear.

"Brown Bear, are you awake?"

Brown Bear sat up in bed. "Yes," he replied. "What's the matter?"

"I've left my favourite teddy at home," whispered Little Bear. "I ALWAYS go to bed with my favourite teddy!"

For a moment Brown Bear thought hard. "Don't worry!" he said, climbing out of bed. "You can borrow my favourite teddy tonight."

"Thank you, Brown Bear!" said Little Bear. He hugged Brown Bear's favourite teddy tightly. "That feels so much better."

Brown Bear climbed back into bed.

"Good night, Little Bear," he called. "Sleep tight!"

"Good night, Brown Bear," called Little Bear.

For a while, everything was quiet.

PITTER PATTER!

PITTER PATTER!

It began to rain. The raindrops fell against the window, lulling the two bears to sleep.

WHOOSH! WHOOSH!

Brown Bear and Little Bear sat up in bed with a start.

"What was that?" squeaked Little Bear, holding on very tightly to Brown Bear's teddy. "And what's that shadow on the wall? Maybe someone is outside!"

Brown Bear pulled back the curtain and peeped out. "Don't be frightened, Little Bear," he said. "It's only the wind in the trees, and the moonlight shining through the window. I'll come and tuck you in."

Brown Bear trotted over and tucked the covers tightly around Little Bear.

"Thank you, Brown Bear," whispered Little Bear, snuggling down again.

"Toowhit! Toowoo! Ttwoo!"

Little Bear dived under his covers. "Oooh!" he shivered. "There *is* something outside! I think it's trying to get in."

Brown Bear chuckled. "Don't worry, Little Bear," he smiled. "It's only Owl!"

Brown Bear pulled back the bedroom curtain. An owl blinked at them through the window.

"Toowhit! Toowoo! Ttwoo!"

he hooted.

"Dear Owl always comes to wish me good night!" explained Brown Bear. "He's a very good friend."

Little Bear giggled. "What a silly billy I am!" he said.

Little Bear and Brown Bear closed the curtain and then climbed back into bed.

"Do you need anything else, Little Bear?" asked Brown Bear kindly.

Little Bear thought for a moment. "I am a bit thirsty," he said.

"I'll get you a drink," offered Brown Bear. "I've got my beaker here."

Brown Bear jumped out of bed and

trotted off to the bathroom. He was soon back with some water for Little Bear.

"Thank you, Brown Bear," whispered Little Bear, sipping his drink. "That's much better."

Brown Bear climbed into bed and pulled up his covers.

"Good night, Little Bear," he sighed. "Sleep tight!"

He was just falling asleep when he heard a small snuffly noise.

SNIFF! SNIFF! SNIFF!

"Is that you, Little Bear?" asked Brown Bear, sitting up in bed. "Whatever is the matter?"

Little Bear sniffed again. "I'm sorry, Brown Bear," he whispered. "It's very dark in here. I'm scared."

Brown Bear thought for a moment. "Don't worry, Little Bear!" he said. "I've got just the answer."

CLICK! Brown Bear switched on his torch and gave it to Little Bear. "You can keep it by your bed," he explained. "Then you can see in the dark."

"Oh, thank you, Brown Bear!" cried Little Bear. "Now I can see where you are."

He shone the torch at Brown Bear's face and waved. Brown Bear waved back. Then he pulled a funny face. Little Bear giggled.

"You look silly," he whispered.

Little Bear put the torch on his bedside table. He snuggled down under his blankets again.

"I'm not scared any more," he said, hugging Brown Bear's teddy tightly. "Good night, Brown Bear."

"Good night, Little Bear!" yawned Brown Bear, plumping his pillow. "Sleep tight!"

For a while, everything was quiet. So quiet, you could hear a pin drop. Then suddenly, a small voice piped up.

"Brown Bear, are you awake?" It was Little Bear.

Brown Bear slowly opened one eye. "Now what's the matter, Little Bear?" he yawned.

"Oh, nothing!" whispered Little Bear. "I just wanted to say thank you for looking after me."

Brown Bear smiled. "That's all right, Little Bear," he said. "That's what bigger bears are for!"

The next morning, Little Bear's daddy arrived bright and early. He gave Little Bear a great big bear hug.

"You've got a new baby sister," he told him. "Are you ready to go and see Mummy and the baby?"

"Oh yes!" cried Little Bear. "Can we go

right now? I can't wait!"

Little Bear's daddy laughed. "Of course," he smiled. "They can't wait to see you either!"

"Can I play with the baby?" asked Little Bear, as they walked along the path. "Can I give her one of my sweets?"

Daddy smiled. "Newborn babies are tiny," he explained. "She's too small to play with you yet. And she only drinks milk at the moment."

Little Bear frowned. "She doesn't sound like much fun," he said.

At the hospital, Mummy was sitting up in bed waiting for them.

"Come and meet Tiny Bear," she whispered. "She's your sister."

Little Bear peeped in the cot.

"She's so small!" he gasped. "I'm much bigger than her!"

"That's right," said Mummy. "You're her big brother."

"I am, aren't I?" said Little Bear proudly. He reached into the cot and took hold of her paw.

"Don't worry, Tiny," he told his little sister. "I'll look after you. After all, that's what bigger bears are for!"

Treasure Trouble

Dragons love to collect treasure. It makes them very happy. There is nothing a dragon loves more than to see a huge pile of treasure glinting and gleaming in the light of his fiery breath. And gold, silver and jewels are the best treasure of all. Treasure hunting is the most important thing a dragon ever learns to do. And dragons are some of the best treasure hunters in the world. At least, most of them are…

Not so long ago, there was a young dragon named Mildy. He was a very nice dragon and his mother loved him very much. But there was one big problem. Mildy knew nothing about treasure.

"I am going to send you to stay with your uncle," said his mother one day. "He is the best treasure hunter in the family. He will teach you everything you need to know."

So Mildy packed his rucksack with some snacks and a picture of his mother, and set off for Uncle Walpu's mountain. Uncle Walpu was happy to help. He was going to teach his nephew all his treasure-hunting secrets.

The first things that Uncle Walpu taught Mildy were the different ways of treasure hunting.

"Treasure is always locked away," said Uncle Walpu. "Sometimes you have to get past huge locks and giant bolts."

Uncle Walpu told Mildy how to break into vaults, dungeons, banks and strongrooms. He explained how to open locks using claws and teeth. He even told

Mildy how to melt safes with his fiery breath. Mildy was a very good pupil. He listened to everything he was told.

Next, Uncle Walpu talked about the safest ways to carry treasure away. This can be tricky when you are flying, so dragons always find a bag or a net to put the treasure in. Mildy practised flying holding rocks and branches, until he was quite sure he could do it.

"If you have to choose between taking treasure or being able to make a safe get-away, leave the treasure behind," said Uncle Walpu. "You can always go back for it another time. It really is better to be safe than sorry."

Mildy nodded wisely. He thought that treasure hunting sounded quite easy. He did some more practice runs, where he had to decide how much to carry. At last, Uncle Walpu said that he was ready. It was time for Mildy to go out on his first treasure-hunting raid.

"There's a castle near here where an old duke lives," said Uncle Walpu. "I have heard that he has a room full of gold and jewels. It's easy to get in and out. The doors are never locked, and the old duke is very mean. He doesn't like paying money to anyone. So he doesn't have many guards. You shouldn't have any trouble. Keep your wits about you and remember all your lessons. And bring back some treasure for me, too!"

Mildy flew off, feeling nervous and excited. Back in

the cave, Uncle Walpu paced up and down. He hoped that his young nephew would find some treasure this first time. The mission was easy. It should be no problem for Mildy. But you never knew with a young dragon. They could panic in a crisis.

But Uncle Walpu shouldn't have worried. In less than an hour, Mildy came flying back. He was carrying a big bag in his claws. The bag was bulging with treasure. Uncle Walpu's eyes shone as his nephew dropped the bag on the floor of the cave.

"Any problems, lad?" he asked.

"It was easy," said Mildy. "Everything was in a big building outside the castle. I didn't have to go anywhere near the duke. There were no locks or guards or dungeons. And just look what I've got!"

Mildy opened the big bag he had

dropped on the floor. Uncle Walpu looked at the shining objects that fell out. They clattered and spun on the floor of the cave. Uncle Walpu couldn't believe his eyes.

"Mildy!" he cried. "What have you done? These are...these are...headlights! These are headlights from cars!"

It was true. Clattering around the floor were twenty shiny car headlights. They were from very expensive cars. But it didn't make any difference to Uncle Walpu. They were headlights all the same.

"Why did you bring these?" asked Uncle Walpu. He felt a bit dizzy with the shock.

"They're shiny," said Mildy. "Aren't they treasure, then?"

Uncle Walpu counted to 80. Then he counted to 100. He could see that he had forgotten to teach Mildy some important things. His nephew would have to be taught what treasure looked like. Uncle Walpu had never known anything like it. All dragons are born knowing about treasure, aren't they?

Uncle Walpu spent three weeks teaching Mildy about treasure. He told him all about the special marks that show you whether gold and silver are real. He taught him how to pick out the best jewels. He taught him about the most expensive gems. He gave Mildy a list of the top ten best items of treasure. Then he gave him a list of the top 100 best items of treasure, just to be sure.

At last, Uncle Walpu felt that Mildy could try again. He had taught him all he knew about jewels, gold and silver. Surely, now, the young dragon was ready?

Mildy flew off to the castle again. This time he went at night.

"Go straight to the castle," said Uncle

Walpu. "Land on the roof. You know what to do, Mildy."

Uncle Walpu was sure that Mildy would find lots of treasure this time. But things did not go well.

The missing headlights had scared the old duke. He thought that whoever had stolen the headlights might come back. They might steal something else. As you know, the duke didn't like spending money. But he didn't want to be burgled either. So he hired six men with fierce dogs to walk around the grounds at night. He bought the very latest alarm system for his castle too.

"No burglar will get past that!" laughed the duke.

But he didn't know what sort of burglar he had. Alarm systems do not usually think that burglars are going to fly in from the air. Mildy landed on the roof without being seen. He did some fiery breathing on the lead of the roof. Soon he had made a hole large enough to squeeze through. Then he climbed into the top of the castle.

Mildy's plan was to sneak all the way down the main stairs to the cellars. He knew that was where most of the gold and silver was kept. He had not thought that there might be anything worth stealing in the upstairs rooms. But Mildy was surprised to see lots of square, shiny things stacked in a corner. He didn't know that they were gold-coloured picture frames. He didn't know that the pictures of old-fashioned people were worth a lot of money. He just loved the shiny frames.

You see, there was something Uncle Walpu did not know. He had told Mildy over and over again that everything that glitters is not gold. He had told the young dragon always to look for a hallmark. That would prove it was real treasure. But he didn't know how much Mildy loved shiny things. As long as it was shiny, Mildy wanted it. He didn't care if it was treasure.

Mildy's eyes opened very wide when he saw the big golden frames. All his lessons went right out of his head.

"So shiny!" he whispered. "So pretty!"

He felt sure that they must be worth something. And they weren't attached to any kind of car, so that must be good. He had learned his lesson about headlights.

Mildy found some rope in a corner. Then he tied the pictures together. He clutched the rope with his claws and launched himself out of the hole in the roof. So far, so good. But he had never practised tying a rope before. Uncle Walpu had not thought about teaching him how to do knots.

As Mildy flew over the castle courtyard, one of the smaller paintings slipped from the bundle. It fell down, down, down onto the flagstones below.

"Oh no!" cried Mildy.

As the picture passed the top windows of the castle, the famous alarm system went off. There was a horrid noise of bells and sirens all around. Poor Mildy was very scared. A second later, he was caught in the glare of ten searchlights. The lights blinded him and he didn't know what to do. He hovered over the castle courtyard.

"Help!" he shouted. But Uncle Walpu was too far away to hear him.

Castle guards are used to some pretty strange things. They see all sorts of odd burglars. They see some strange visitors coming to the castle. But they hardly ever see a flying dragon. The duke's guards stood staring at the dragon above them. They all had their mouths open. Even the dogs forgot to bark.

The duke heard all the noise. He came running out of the castle and looked up as well. He didn't care that it was a dragon. He just cared about his paintings.

"Shoot it!" he cried.

Mildy had no idea what this meant. But he knew a mean and nasty voice when he heard it. He blinked a few times and remembered what Uncle Walpu had told him.

"If you have to choose between taking treasure or being able to make a safe get-away, leave the treasure behind."

Mildy dropped the bundle of pictures. Then he flew off to the mountains as fast as his wings could carry him. The big pile of pictures fell like a stone and hit the nasty duke on the head.

Back at his cave, Uncle Walpu was waiting to find out what had happened. He was almost knocked off his feet by Mildy's landing. Mildy rolled over and over and stopped at the back of the cave. Uncle Walpu sighed. He didn't need to be told that something had gone very wrong.

It took Mildy a long time to pant out his story. It took Uncle Walpu even longer to work out what had really happened, because Mildy did not understand about searchlights. He thought they were monsters with big eyes. He didn't understand about alarm bells either. He said that the monsters had shouted at him in horrible high voices.

Uncle Walpu picked out the only important point from all the panting and the stories about monsters.

"What you tried to steal, Mildy, were pictures," he said crossly. "Look at me, now. Are they on the list of the top ten best items of treasure?"

"No," said Mildy sadly.

"Are they even on the list of the top 100 best items of treasure?"

"No."

"So why did you try to steal them then?" asked Uncle Walpu.

"Because they were so shiny," said Mildy, hanging his head.

Uncle Walpu lost his temper. "Windows are shiny!" he roared. "Bald heads are shiny! But should you try to steal them? NO! It is so simple, Mildy, that even a human could understand it. Gold, silver and jewels. Silver, gold and jewels. Gold, jewels and silver. It doesn't matter which way round you say it. There are only three things worth stealing. What are they?"

"Sold, jilder and gewels," said Mildy unhappily. He felt very confused.

His uncle gave a sigh that set fire to a forest three miles away. Then he flapped off into the night to cool his temper.

When he felt calmer, Uncle Walpu sat down and wrote out a plan for Mildy's training. It was very long. It covered the most basic rules of treasure hunting. It was so easy that most young dragons would have laughed to see it. But it was at just the right level for Mildy. Uncle Walpu decided that he would try to stay as calm as he could. Then he got ready to do the training.

Uncle Walpu did his best. But it was hopeless. Mildy understood what he was supposed to do. But, as soon as he tried to do it, everything went wrong.

Mildy broke the tower of a local church when he tried to steal a shiny weather vane.

A week later, he got locked in the

vaults of the local bank. Uncle Walpu rescued him just in time.

And the week after that, Mildy raided a jeweller's shop and came home with five plastic rubies. He just couldn't tell the difference between real jewels and fake ones.

Every time Mildy did something silly (which was quite often), Uncle Walpu took a few days off to calm down. While he was waiting, Mildy walked around the mountainside and paddled in the cold, clear streams. He liked kicking the rocks to make tiny landslides. But then one of the landslides almost blocked up the entrance to Uncle Walpu's cave – while Uncle Walpu was inside it. After that, Mildy was not allowed to go outside by himself. So he wandered around the caves inside the mountain, kicking at the walls and sighing. The cave walls were full of foot-shaped holes.

Uncle Walpu tried for six long months. He did everything he could. He even went treasure hunting with Mildy. Dragons are not supposed to fly around together, but this was an emergency.

Mildy was fine when his uncle came along with him. It was easy when he had someone to tell him what to do. He could steal anything when he had that kind of help. The problems came when he went out on his own. Mildy went to pieces. He didn't think. He didn't plan. He didn't use his head at all. He just picked up anything shiny, no matter what it was.

Uncle Walpu had thought that he was a good teacher. But at last he had to admit that he had failed.

"Mildy," he said, "I am going to send you back to your mother. It breaks my heart to let her down. She wanted me to teach you all I know. But I have to stop now. I've spent so much time teaching you that I haven't found any treasure for myself. I've done all that I can for you. You will never have treasure of your own and that is the end of it."

Mildy hung his head.

"I'm sorry," he said. "I have really tried hard. I just can't remember all the rules. I can't understand why gold and silver and jewels don't count as treasure when you find them the easy way."

"What are you talking about?" asked Uncle Walpu. "What easy way is there?"

"I mean the treasure that is just sitting in the mountains, waiting to be found," said Mildy. "Don't you know where it is? Look, I'll show you!"

He led his uncle deep, deep into the cave. Then he kicked at a wall, just like he had been doing for months. Something sparkled and fell to the ground. Something else glittered in the wall. They were diamonds!

"Diamonds!" cried Uncle Walpu. "Right here in my cave!"

"There's more," said Mildy. He took his uncle outside to a stream. Mildy showed Uncle Walpu lots of little pieces of gold. He had found them all in the streams on the mountain.

Uncle Walpu could hardly believe his eyes. He smiled slowly.

"I was wrong about you, young Mildy,"

he said. "Of course this is real treasure. I don't know why we dragons go flying and stealing when all this is here...right under our dragon noses. I really don't have anything left to teach you. Go home and tell your mother that she should be proud of you."

"Couldn't I just stay a few more days?" asked Mildy.

"Certainly not!" laughed Uncle Walpu. "The diamonds and gold on this mountain are all mine!"

A Very Spotty Birthday

It was bedtime, but Jake was far too excited to go to sleep. Every time he closed his eyes, all he could think about was the next morning – Saturday morning – when he would be five years old.

Jake had everything planned. First of all, he would go downstairs in his pyjamas, and watch his favourite cartoons, eating chocolate pops on the sofa. No one would say, "Get dressed, Jake," or "Eat your breakfast at the table, Jake," because it was his birthday. And everyone knows you're allowed to do what you like on your birthday.

Then, when he felt like it, and not before, he would get dressed. He was going to wear his favourite red tracksuit and old blue T-shirt. And no one would say, "Not those old clothes again!" because everyone knows you're allowed to wear what you like on your birthday.

The postman would deliver a huge pile of cards, all addressed to Jake, and he would open them, one by one, very s...l...o...w...l...y. He wouldn't have to go to school. He wouldn't have to tidy his bedroom, and he wouldn't have to do anything he didn't want to, because it was HIS birthday! After lunch, Jake's friends were coming round for his birthday party! They were going to have a picnic in the park, then go rollerblading. Jake was getting a pair of rollerblades for his birthday, and he couldn't wait to try them out!

"Are you still awake?" whispered Mum, tucking Jake's duvet snugly round his shoulders. "It's a big day tomorrow. You'll need plenty of sleep if you're going to rollerblade all afternoon!"

"But I can't get to sleep," said Jake, pushing back the duvet. "I can't stop thinking about tomorrow. And I'm too hot – my head feels a bit funny."

"I expect it's because you're so excited," said Mum, feeling his forehead. "I'll open the window. Now close your eyes and you'll be fast asleep in no time."

When Jake opened his eyes the next morning, the first thing he saw was a brightly wrapped parcel, propped up at the end of his bed. "Hurray!" he yelled, sitting up in bed excitedly and rubbing his eyes. "It's my birthday!"

Jake reached over to get the parcel, and gave it a careful shake. It was very heavy.

"I bet it's my rollerblades," he cried,

tearing off the wrapping paper, and opening the box.

Jake peered inside the box. It WAS a pair of rollerblades – the shiny red-and-gold ones he had seen in the shop!

"Coooooool!" Jake shouted.

He was just about to put his foot in one of the rollerblades when suddenly his ankle felt very itchy. SCRATCH ! SCRATCH! Jake gave his ankle a good old scratch.

Then he scratched it again. SCRATCH! SCRATCH! And again. But the itch just wouldn't go away.

What was more, his leg was itchy, too...and his elbow...and his bottom...in fact, he was itching all over!

Jake jumped out of bed and ran over to the mirror.

"Oh no!" he gulped, staring at his face. It was covered in spots!

And so were his hands...and his elbows...and his neck...

"Mum!" shouted Jake.

"Goodness!" cried Mum, when she saw Jake. "I think you'd better go back to bed. You're spotty all over. I'll call the doctor."

Jake groaned. "But it's my birthday!" he said, trying not to feel too disappointed. "I wanted to go downstairs in my pyjamas and eat my breakfast watching cartoons."

"We can do even better than that!"

said Dad, coming up the stairs. "We'll bring the cartoons and breakfast to you instead. Hop back into bed, and I'll set up the television in your bedroom."

"WOW!" grinned Jake.

While Jake watched his cartoons in bed, Mum phoned the doctor's surgery. Half an hour later, Doctor Blythe arrived.

"Now then, Jake. What's the problem?" she asked kindly.

"I'm spotty all over!" replied Jake, showing the doctor his spots.

"I can see that," said Doctor Blythe, smiling. "That's because you've got chicken pox."

She reached in her bag, pulled out a notepad and wrote something on the top sheet. Then she gave the sheet to Mum.

"You will need some special lotion to stop the itching," Doctor Blythe told Jake. "This will tell the chemist what to give you."

"Can I still have my birthday party today?" Jake asked hopefully. "We're going rollerblading in the park."

Doctor Blythe shook her head. "I'm sorry, Jake," she said. "You can't play with your friends just yet. Otherwise, they'll catch chicken pox too."

Jake's bottom lip wobbled. "It's not fair," he whispered. "It's my birthday."

Dad tried to cheer him up. "I'll take you rollerblading as soon as you're better," he promised.

"Thanks," mumbled Jake into his duvet. "But it won't be the same."

When Doctor Blythe had gone, Mum came back upstairs to check on Jake.

"We'll just have to try and make the day as fun as we can," said Mum, squeezing his hand. "But first I'll have to ring your friends and tell them the party is cancelled."

Jake listened to Mum's footsteps going down the stairs. "How can my birthday be fun now?" he thought. "Everything is spoiled!"

He closed his eyes and before long he had fallen fast asleep.

DING! DONG!

The doorbell rang loudly and Jake awoke with a jump. He felt much better.

"Who's at the door?" he wondered,

sitting up in bed.

Just then, Jake heard lots of giggling on the landing outside his bedroom door.

"Who's that?" he called. "What's going on?"

"It's Mum and Dad," came the reply. "We've got a surprise for you."

The bedroom door burst open, and in stepped Jake's best friends, Molly and Ben.

"What are you doing here?" asked Jake. Then he began to giggle. Molly's and Ben's faces were covered in spots too.

"We've got chicken pox, just like you," they grinned, showing off their spotty arms.

"You must have caught it from each other," said Mum. "When I rang Molly and Ben to say you had chicken pox, Molly's mum and Ben's mum said they had it too. So we decided you could have a party after all. They can't catch chicken pox from you if they've already got it!"

"Hurray!" yelled Jake, bouncing up and down on his bed. "I'm having a birthday party!" Then he stopped bouncing. "But what are we going to *do* at my party?" he asked. "We can't go rollerblading, can we?"

"This is going to be a special spotty party!" replied Dad. "And the first game we're going to play is called 'Painting Spots'!"

Dad handed each of them a small bottle of pink lotion and a cotton-wool ball.

"Doctor Blythe said you have to paint this on your spots, to stop them itching," he said. Then he looked at his watch. "You have just five minutes to see how many spots you can paint. Are you ready? On your marks, get set, go!"

WHAT A MESS! Pink lotion splattered everywhere as the three spotty children tried to paint as many of their spots as they could.

They painted their cheeks...

They painted their feet...

They painted their ears...

They even painted their noses...

They looked more like pink marshmallows than children with chicken pox.

"STOP!" cried Dad, holding up his hand. "Your time is up!" He examined the three children. "And the winner is...Molly, by two toes!" he announced, handing over the prize – a huge lolly with red spots.

Next they played 'Count the Spots'. Then they played 'Spot the Difference' and did dot-to-dot puzzles. Everyone was having so much fun that they forgot about feeling hot and itchy. Jake even forgot about roller-blading.

They had just finished sticking coloured spots on their party hats, when Mum put her head around the door.

"Are you hungry yet?" she asked. Molly, Ben and Jake all nodded.

"It's just that I thought you might want a SPOT of something to eat," she joked, carrying in a big tray of food. There were squares of cheese on toast with tomato sauce spots...there were glasses of milkshake with lots of dots all over them...and there was an enormous chocolate cake covered with red sweets.

After they had eaten, Jake opened his presents and cards. He had a pair of rollerblading gloves to protect his hands and a set of elbow protectors from Ben.

"COOOL!" exclaimed Jake, trying them on. "Do you want to see my rollerblades?" He opened the box and carefully lifted out his brand-new blades.

"WOW!" cried Molly and Ben together. Then they both began to laugh.

"What's so funny?" asked Jake, looking at his boots. Then he started to laugh too. He hadn't noticed before, but his new red rollerblades were covered in gold spots. The perfect gift for a very spotty birthday!

"Did you have a fun time today?" asked Dad, tucking Jake up in bed that night.

"It was my best birthday ever," replied Jake.

"Even though you didn't go rollerblading?" asked Mum.

Jake smiled. "I can go rollerblading any day," he said. "But hardly anyone gets to have a very spotty birthday!"